The Truth in the Meadow

Written by Sara Sams

Illustrated by Gudrød Veidekonge

*Dedicated to every heart that may forget
the truth in the meadow from time to time.*

"You are just as
you should be!"

xo
Sara Sams

At the edge of the meadow where the thistles smell sweet stood a Little One full of wonder. The Little One was often caught wondering about many things. Especially why things were the way they were. She wondered why her curly wild hair wasn't straight. Why freckles dotted her face.

Why rivers flow downhill. Why trees grow this way and that. "Shouldn't things be different or better?" She wondered. It was with these thoughts that she began her stroll through the tree lined meadow where the thistles smell sweet.

A few moments later the Little One came across a bunny. The bunny busily built her burrow, hopping this way and that. She kicked soil from the sides of the tree roots creating a safe home for her bunnies. She fetched feathers, leaves, and twigs, making it as cozy and comfy as she could.

"Skip! Little bunny!" Demanded the Little One. "But I hop, hop, hop."
"You should skip. It would be better!"
"I should hop because I hop." Stated the bunny and happily hopped away.
"Hmm." She thought and continued on her way.

Soon a goose crossed her path. The powerful goose was preparing for her long trip to warmer weather. Every winter she left the cold behind and summered in warmer woods. She patiently listened for the honking of the geese she would fly with. Just then, the goose heard the honking flock fly overhead.
"Honk! Honk! Honk!" She sang in excitement.

"Sing! Honking goose." Said the Little One.
"Honking is my song." Declared the goose.
"You should sing. It would be better."
"I honk Little One. Honk! Honk! Honk!" She replied and
powerfully took off to join her V of friends in the sky.
"Hmm." She thought and continued on her way.

While skipping along the pebbled path, she discovered a prickly porcupine climbing down a nearby tree. The porcupine made his home in trees to stay safe from foxes and other critters. His quills kept him safe, too. Should he find himself in harms way, he would definitely use his quills to defend himself, but he loved them far too much to give them to a sly fox or creeping coyote.

"You should be soft and smooth; not so prickly!" Opined the Little One.
"But I'm prickly, prickly, prickly." Defended the porcupine and without any more fuss, fluffed his quills and proudly waddled away in search of a tasty twig to munch.
"Hmm." She thought and continued on her way.

As the Little One meandered through the grass she came upon a field mouse puposefully gathering items. The mouse squeaked happily as he discovered feathers, bark, and twigs to build his nest.

"You should be quiet and stop squeak, squeak, squeaking!" Said the Little One.

"Sometimes I am quiet. Sometimes I squeak." Said the mouse and scurried away.

"Hmm." She thought and continued on her way.

After so much walking, the Little One decided to lay in the cool grass. As she did a skunk scuttled by. The skunk had just defended her kits with her powerful potent perfume from a farm dog who dared come too close.

The Little One sniffed the air and said, "You smell sour. You should smell sweetly."

"I smell like I smell." Whispered the skunk and sweetly padded on knowing the Little One didn't quite understand the truth of it all.

"Hmm." She thought and continued to lay in the grass.

As the Little One lay in the meadow she thought of all the critters she'd met that day and wondered if they were just as they should be...
The sun settled deeper in the sky. It was time for the Little One to head home.

On her way back she ran into the skunk. She thought of the skunk's bravery and how her stinky spray kept her family safe. She bent and said, "You are just as you should be!"
The skunk nodded and quickly padded on with her kits following behind.

As the crickets began to sing, the Little One saw the field mouse gathering seeds noisily. She remembered the field mouse happily collecting items for colder times. Squeaking was the mouse's joyful noise.

She bent and said, "You are just as you should be!"

The field mouse nodded and scurried on.

Skipping down the path she saw the porcupine. The Little One recalled his prickly quills' protecting power.

She bent and said, "You are just as you should be!"

The porcupine nodded, fluffed his quills, and proudly waddled away.

Soon she heard the honking goose fly above. She was now impressed with the powerful song she heard, knowing it would make it possible for the goose to fly safely south.
She bent back and happily yelled into the sky,
"You are just as you should be!"
The goose nodded, honked even louder, and powerfully flew away.

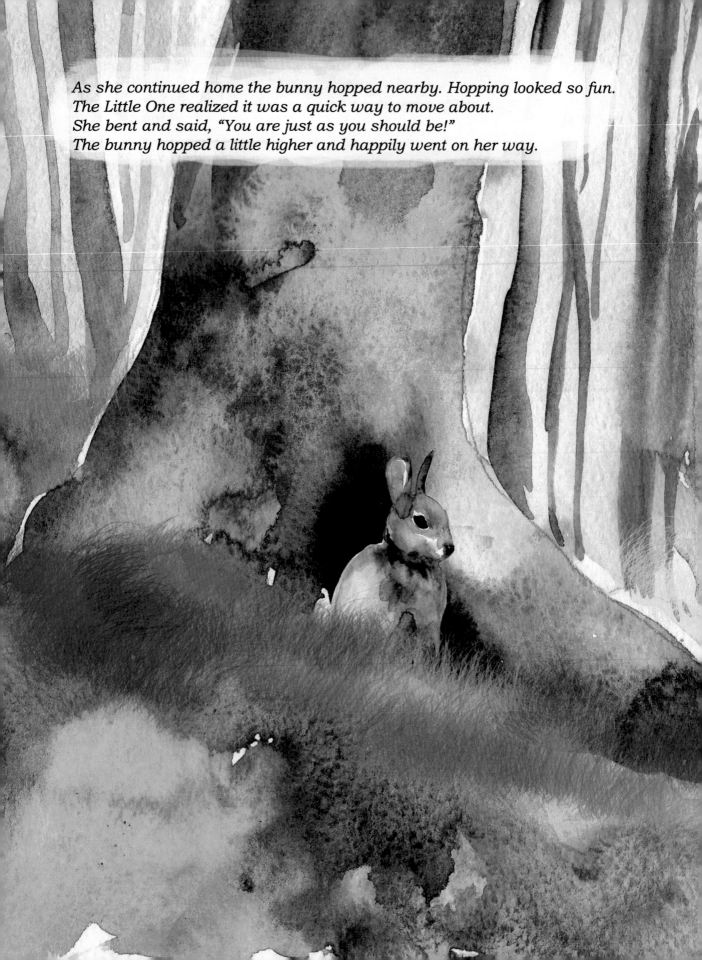

As she continued home the bunny hopped nearby. Hopping looked so fun.
The Little One realized it was a quick way to move about.
She bent and said, "You are just as you should be!"
The bunny hopped a little higher and happily went on her way.

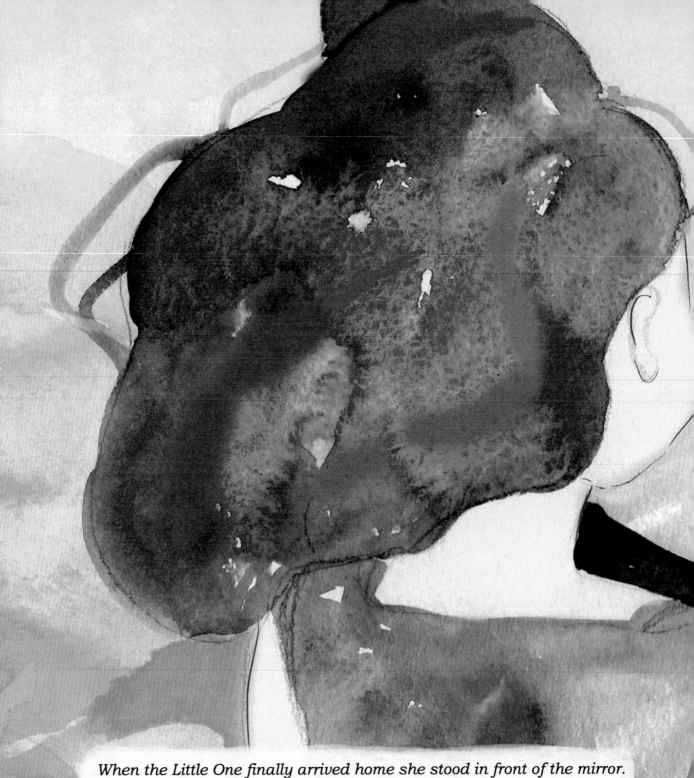

When the Little One finally arrived home she stood in front of the mirror. She gazed at her reflection and said, "You should be..."
Pausing for a moment, she thought of the critters she encountered that day. A twinkle entered her eye and a smile spread across her face. The freckles she wasn't pleased with earlier now looked like stars kissing her cheeks and she liked that.

When she looked at her wild hair, she found blossoms hidden in the curls reminding her of the day's adventure and she liked that, too. She realized the truth of it all and said, "You are just as you should be!"
With that, she fluffed her wild curls, loved her freckles a little more, and continued on her way.

Made in the USA
San Bernardino, CA
26 April 2016